P9-CQR-569

More from

WALTER DEAN MYERS

and HarperCollins Publishers

Juba!

Darius & Twig

The Get Over
(available as e-book only)

Tags
(available as e-book only)

Just Write: Here's How!

All the Right Stuff

We Are America: A Tribute from the Heart
Illustrated by Christopher Myers

Kick
Coauthored by Ross Workman

Looking for the Easy Life
Illustrated by Lee Harper

Lockdown

Muhammad Ali: The People's Champion
Illustrated by Alix Delinois

Dope Sick

Game

Ida B. Wells: Let the Truth Be Told
Illustrated by Bonnie Christensen

Harlem Hellfighters: When Pride Met Courage

Street Love

Autobiography of My Dead Brother
Illustrated by Christopher Myers

I've Seen the Promised Land:
The Life of Dr. Martin Luther King, Jr.

Shooter

The Dream Bearer

Handbook for Boys: A Novel

Patrol: An American Soldier in Vietnam
Illustrated by Ann Grifalconi

Bad Boy: A Memoir

Malcolm X: A Fire Burning Brightly

Monster

Angel to Angel

Glorious Angels: An Album of Pictures and Verse

The Story of the Three Kingdoms
Illustrated by Ashley Bryan

Brown Angels: An Album of Pictures and Verse

The Righteous Revenge of Artemis Bonner

Now Is Your Time!: The African-American Struggle for Freedom

The Mouse Rap

Scorpions

Tales of a Dead King

Amistad is an imprint of HarperCollins Publishers.

Monster: A Graphic Novel
Text copyright © 1999 by Walter Dean Myers
and © 2015 by the Estate of Walter Myers
Illustrations copyright © 2015 by Dawud Anyabwile
All rights reserved. Manufactured in China.
No part of this book may be used or reproduced in any manner whatsoever without written
permission except in the case of brief quotations embodied in critical articles and reviews.
For information address HarperCollins Children's Books,
a division of HarperCollins Publishers, 195 Broadway, New York, NY 10007.
www.epicreads.com

Library of Congress Cataloging-in-Publication Data
Sims, Guy A.
    Monster: a graphic novel / by Walter Dean Myers ; adapted by Guy A. Sims ; illustrated by Dawud
Anyabwile. — First edition.
        pages   cm
    Summary: While on trial as an accomplice to a murder, sixteen-year-old Steve Harmon records his
experiences in prison and in the courtroom in the form of a film script as he tries to come to terms with
the course his life has taken.
    ISBN 978-0-06-227500-4 (hardcover)
    ISBN 978-0-06-227499-1 (pbk.)
    1. Graphic novels.   [1. Graphic novels.   2. Trials (Murder)—Fiction.   3. Prisons—Fiction.
4. Self-perception—Fiction.   5. African Americans—Fiction.   6. Myers, Walter Dean, date, Monster—
Adaptations.]   I. Anyabwile, Dawud, date, illustrator.   II. Myers, Walter Dean, date, Monster.   III. Title.
PZ7.7.S547Mo   2015   2013043138
[741.5'973]—dc23   CIP
                                                                                                                        AC

3 1907 00352 3445

The artist used Photoshop to create the digital illustrations for this book.
Typography by Dana Fritts
15 16 17 18 19   SCP   10 9 8 7 6 5 4 3 2 1
❖

MOST PEOPLE IN OUR COMMUNITY ARE **DECENT, HARDWORKING** CITIZENS WHO PURSUE THEIR OWN INTERESTS **LEGALLY** AND WITHOUT INFRINGING ON THE **RIGHTS** OF OTHERS...

...BUT THERE ARE ALSO **MONSTERS** IN OUR COMMUNITIES... PEOPLE WHO ARE **WILLING** TO STEAL AND TO KILL... PEOPLE WHO DISREGARD THE **RIGHTS** OF OTHERS...

2

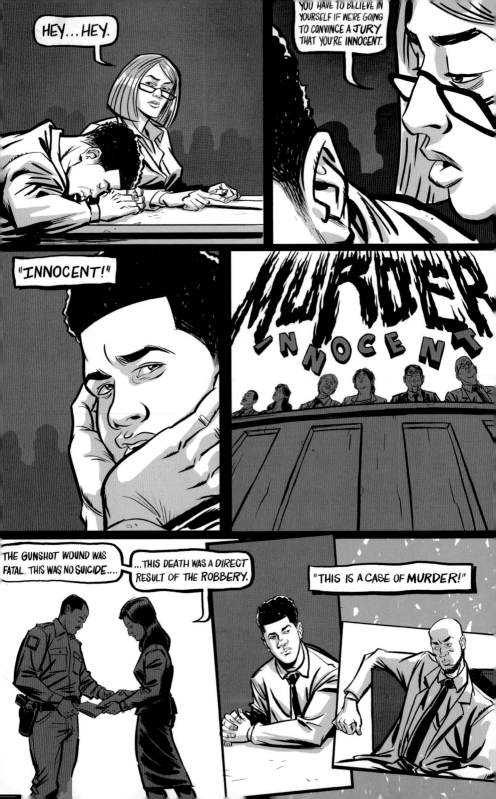

"NOTHING FURTHER."

AFTERWARD... I CHECKED THE INVENTORY. IT WAS 5.

YOU STATE THAT 5 CARTONS OF CIGARETTES WERE MISSING?

THAT'S RIGHT.

5...NOT 6?

WHAT MEDICAL SCHOOL DID YOU ATTEND?

NONE.

BUT YOU SAID YOU KNEW THAT MR. NESBITT WAS DEAD. YOU WERE SURE OF IT?

I'M PRETTY SURE.

"SURE ENOUGH TO STOP AND DO INVENTORY BEFORE TRYING TO HELP YOUR BOSS?"

INVENTORY

I DIDN'T TAKE INVENTORY RIGHT AWAY.... I JUST NOTICED. YOU WORK IN A STORE, YOU NOTICE IF SOMETHING IS MISSING.

"NOTHING FURTHER."

"CALL YOUR NEXT WITNESS, MS. PETROCELLI."

"SO HOW LONG DID IT TAKE?"

NOT LONG.

"THE STATE CALLS MR. WENDELL BOLDEN."

MR. BOLDEN, HAVE YOU EVER BEEN ARRESTED?

YEAH. FOR B AND E... AND FOR POSSESSION WITH INTENT.

POSSESSION IS OBVIOUSLY DRUGS AND THE INTENT TO DISTRIBUTE. CAN YOU TELL THE JURY WHAT B AND E MEANS?

"B AND E ...BREAKING AND ENTERING."

"AND WHAT WERE YOU IN FOR WHEN YOU SPOKE TO MR. ZINZI?"

ASSAULT.

THAT WAS WHAT I WAS THINKING ABOUT, WHAT WAS IN MY HEART AND WHAT THAT MADE ME.

I'M JUST NOT A BAD PERSON.

I KNOW THAT IN MY HEART I AM **NOT** A BAD PERSON.

66

"I'VE **NEVER** SEEN MY FATHER CRY BEFORE. HE WASN'T CRYING LIKE I THOUGHT A MAN WOULD CRY. EVERYTHING WAS JUST POURING OUT OF HIM, AND I HATED TO SEE HIS FACE."

"WHAT DID I DO?"

"WHAT DID I DO?"

71

"I'M GOING TO HAVE TO DO SOME EDITING."

"I CAN'T STOMACH THIS PART OF THE TRIAL."

"IT'S TOO REAL. I'LL START WITH THIS SECTION."

IT WAS A REGISTERED GUN. THAT PERMIT WAS IN EFFECT SINCE 1999.

SO THERE WAS NOTHING UNUSUAL OR ILLEGAL ABOUT THE GUN BEING IN THE DRUGSTORE? IS THAT CORRECT, MR. FORBES?

I ARRIVED AT THE SCENE AT 5:15. THE BODY OF THE VICTIM WAS LYING HALFWAY... HIS LEGS WERE HALF STICKING OUT FROM BEHIND THE COUNTER.

I DIDN'T KNOW AT THE TIME IF IT WAS THE GUN THAT KILLED THE VICTIM OR NOT.

WE CHALKED THE BODY SO WE COULD TURN IT OVER AND SEE IF THERE WAS ANY POSSIBLE EVIDENCE BENEATH THE VICTIM.

THE GUYS AT THE MEDICAL EXAMINER'S OFFICE WANTED TO MOVE THE BODY.

IT WAS TIME FOR THEIR SHIFT TO END...AND I ALLOWED IT.

THE AUTOPSY I CONDUCTED REVEALED A COMBINATION OF TRAUMA TO THE INTERNAL ORGANS... AS WELL AS BY THE LUNGS FILLING WITH BLOOD.

YOU MEAN HE LITERALLY DROWNED IN HIS OWN BLOOD?

"AS MUCH AS I WANT TO. I CAN'T CUT THIS OUT."

"I FINALLY UNDERSTAND WHY THERE ARE SO MANY FIGHTS."

"AND YOU DIDN'T SPEAK TO HIM AFTER THE STICKUP OR SPLIT ANY MONEY WITH HIM?"

"I TOLD YOU WE DECIDED TO LAY LOW. WE WOULD HAVE GIVEN HIM HIS CUT LATER WHEN THINGS COOLED DOWN."

"DID THAT TIME EVER COME?"

"I DON'T KNOW WHAT KING DID."

"BUT AS FAR AS YOU KNOW... THERE WAS NO MONEY GIVEN TO MR. HARMON."

"I DON'T KNOW WHAT KING DONE."

"NOTHING FURTHER."

"THE PEOPLE REST."

"MS. O'BRIEN CAME TO SEE ME THIS AFTERNOON. SHE LOOKED TIRED. SHE SAID THAT BOBO'S TESTIMONY HURT US A LOT...."

"SHE HAS TO FIND A WAY TO SEPARATE ME FROM KING, BUT KING'S LAWYER WANTS TO MAKE SURE THE JURY CONNECTS US, BECAUSE I LOOK LIKE A PRETTY DECENT GUY...."

"I ASKED HER IF SHE THOUGHT WE WERE GOING TO LOSE THE CASE. SHE SAID NO BUT I DON'T BELIEVE HER."

"I AM SO SCARED. MY HEART IS BEATING LIKE CRAZY AND I'M HAVING TROUBLE BREATHING. THE TROUBLE I'M IN KEEPS GETTING BIGGER AND BIGGER. I'M OVERWHELMED BY IT. IT'S CRUSHING ME."

Trust

"TOMORROW WE START OUR CASE AND I DON'T SEE WHAT WE ARE GOING TO DO. LIKE EVERY OTHER PRISONER IN HERE, I TRY TO CONVINCE MYSELF THAT EVERYTHING WILL BE ALL RIGHT...THAT THE JURY CAN'T FIND ME GUILTY BECAUSE OF THIS REASON OR THAT REASON."

"WE LIE TO OURSELVES HERE. MAYBE WE ARE HERE BECAUSE WE LIE TO OURSELVES."

YEAH...KEEP TELLING YOURSELF THAT.

We lie to Ourselves

HAVE YOU EVER SEEN MR. KING SHOOT A MAN?
NO... I HAVEN'T.
"SO WHEN HE SHOOTS A GUN... YOU DON'T KNOW WHAT HAND HE USES."
"IS THAT RIGHT?"
"OBJECTION!"
IF MR. KING WAS STRUGGLING WITH SOMEONE AND THE GUN HAPPENED TO BE ON THE RIGHT SIDE, DO YOU KNOW WHAT HE WOULD DO?
"MR. NIPPING?"
NO... NO I DON'T.
"NOTHING FURTHER."

TRUTH

WHAT IS TRUTH

ANYBODY IN HERE KNOW
WHAT TRUTH IS

TRUTH IS TRUTH

IT'S WHAT YOU KNOW
TO BE RIGHT

OR IS IT SOMETHING
YOU GIVE UP

WHEN YOU'RE
OUT THERE
ON THE
STREETS

"ONE LAST QUESTION. WERE YOU IN ANY WAY INVOLVED WITH THE CRIME THAT WE ARE DISCUSSING HERE? TO MAKE IT CLEAR: WERE YOU...IN ANY WAY...INVOLVED WITH THE HOLDUP AND MURDER THAT OCCURRED ON THE 22ND OF DECEMBER?"
NO. I WAS NOT.
"NOTHING FURTHER. MS. PETROCELLI."

TAKE
DEEP
BREATHS

"THE DEFENSE CALLS GEORGE SAWICKI!"

"...I BELIEVE THAT JUSTICE DEMANDS THAT YOU REJECT THE TESTIMONY OF THESE MEN... CONSIGNING THEIR STORIES TO THE AREA OF DEEP DOUBT.... I BELIEVE THAT JUSTICE DEMANDS THAT YOU RETURN A VERDICT OF **NOT GUILTY.**"

"... IT'S UP TO YOU... THE JURY... TO FIND **GUILT** WHERE THERE IS **GUILT.** IT IS ALSO UP TO YOU TO ACQUIT WHEN GUILT HAS NOT BEEN PROVEN. THERE IS NO QUESTION IN MY MIND THAT IN THIS CASE... AS REGARDS **STEVE HARMON...** GUILT HAS NOT BEEN PROVEN. I AM ASKING YOU... ON BEHALF OF **STEVE HARMON**... AND IN THE NAME OF **JUSTICE**... TO CLOSELY CONSIDER ALL OF THE EVIDENCE THAT YOU HAVE HEARD DURING THIS LAST WEEK. IF YOU DO..., I'M SURE YOU'LL RETURN A VERDICT OF **NOT GUILTY**... AND THAT WILL BE THE **RIGHT** THING TO DO...."

"... MR. HARMON WAS INVOLVED. HE MADE A MORAL DECISION TO PARTICIPATE IN THIS 'GET OVER.' HE WANTED TO 'GET PAID' LIKE EVERYBODY ELSE. HE IS AS GUILTY AS EVERYBODY ELSE... NO MATTER HOW MANY MORAL HAIRS HE CAN SPLIT. HIS PARTICIPATION MADE THE CRIME EASIER. HIS WILLINGNESS TO CHECK OUT THE STORE... NO MATTER HOW POORLY HE DID IT... WAS ONE OF THOSE CAUSATIVE FACTORS THAT RESULTED IN THE DEATH OF **MR. NESBITT.** NONE OF US CAN BRING BACK **MR. NESBITT.** NONE OF US CAN RESTORE HIM TO HIS FAMILY... BUT THE 12 OF YOU... YOU 12 CITIZENS OF OUR STATE... OF OUR CITY... CAN BRING A MEASURE OF JUSTICE TO HIS KILLERS, AND THAT'S ALL I ASK OF YOU... TO REACH INTO YOUR HEARTS AND MINDS AND BRING FORTH A MEASURE OF **JUSTICE**...."

"LAST NIGHT I WAS AFRAID TO GO TO SLEEP. IT WAS AS IF CLOSING MY EYES WAS GOING TO CAUSE ME TO DIE."

"THERE IS NOTHING MORE FOR ME TO DO."

"THERE ARE NO MORE ARGUMENTS TO MAKE. NOW I UNDERSTAND WHY SO MANY OF THE GUYS WHO HAVE BEEN THROUGH IT BEFORE...WHO HAVE BEEN AWAY TO PRISON...KEEP TALKING ABOUT APPEALS."

"THEY WANT TO CONTINUE THE ARGUMENT...AND THE SYSTEM HAS SAID THAT IT IS OVER."

"MY CASE FILLS ME. WHEN I LEFT THE COURTROOM AFTER THE JUDGE'S INSTRUCTIONS, I SAW MAMA CLINGING TO MY FATHER'S ARM. THERE WAS A LOOK OF DESPERATION ON HER FACE. FOR A MOMENT I FELT SORRY FOR HER...BUT I DON'T ANYMORE."

"THE ONLY THING I CAN THINK OF IS MY CASE. I LISTEN TO GUYS TALKING ABOUT APPEALS AND I AM ALREADY PLANNING MINE."

"EVERY WORD THAT HAS BEEN SAID IN COURT IS BURNED INTO MY BRAIN. 'STEVE HARMON MADE A MORAL DECISION,' MS. PETROCELLI SAID. I THINK ABOUT DECEMBER OF LAST YEAR. WHAT WAS THE DECISION I MADE? TO WALK DOWN THE STREETS? TO GET UP IN THE MORNING? TO TALK TO KING? WHAT DECISIONS DID I MAKE? WHAT DECISIONS DIDN'T I MAKE? BUT I DON'T WANT TO THINK ABOUT DECISIONS...JUST MY CASE."

"...JUST MY CASE."

"NOTHING IS REAL AROUND ME EXCEPT THE PANIC. THE PANIC AND THE MOVIES THAT DANCE THROUGH MY MIND. I KEEP EDITING THE MOVIES...MAKING THE SCENE RIGHT...SHARPENING THE DIALOGUE. A 'GETOVER'? I DON'T DO 'GETOVERS.'"

"IN THE MOVIE IN MY MIND, MY CHIN IS TILTED SLIGHTLY UPWARD. I KNOW WHAT RIGHT IS...WHAT TRUTH IS. I HAVE NO DOUBTS...MORAL OR OTHERWISE."

"I PUT STRINGS IN THE BACKGROUND... CELLOS...VIOLAS...."

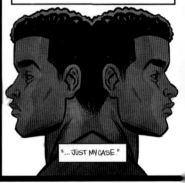

This is the true story of Steve Harmon. This is the story of his life and of his trial.

It was not an episode that he expected. It was not the life or activity that he thought would fill every bit of his soul or change what life meant to him.

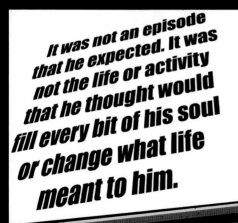

He has transcribed the images and conversations as he remembers them.